SCHOLASTIC

Fun With Phonics!

Beginning Consonants

by Deborah Eaton

SCHOLASTIC
PROFESSIONAL BOOKS

NEW YORK • TORONTO • LONDON • AUCKLAND • SYDNEY

Dear Teacher,

Nothing can be more important in the primary grades than instilling in children the joy of reading and teaching them the skills to become successful, lifelong readers. To do this, we must teach children how to unlock the mysteries of print. Reading instruction that includes systematic and explicit phonics instruction is essential to achieve this goal.

Phonics instruction unlocks the door to understanding sounds and the letters or spelling patterns that represent them. Quality phonics instruction engages children, provides opportunities for them to think about how words work, and offers reading and writing experiences for children to apply their developing skills. The playful, purposeful activities in the *Fun With Phonics!* series offer practice, reinforcement, and assessment of phonics skills. In combination with your daily reading instruction, these activities will help to capture the fun and excitement associated with learning to read.

Enjoy!

Wiley Blevins, Reading Specialist

Cover Design: Vincent Ceci, Liza Charlesworth, and Jaime Lucero
Cover Illustration: Abby Carter

Series Development by Brown Publishing Network, Inc.
Editorial: Elinor Chamas
Interior Design and Production: Diana Maloney and Kathy Meisl

Interior Illustrations: Shelly Dieterichs

Contents

Using "Fun With Phonics!" — 4

Family Letter — 5

Poem *Letters on the Run* — 6

Roll-a-Letter *Beginning Consonants* **Ff, Hh, Jj, Nn, Pp, Ww** — 7

Gift Boxes *Beginning Consonants* **Ll, Mm, Ss, Tt** — 8

Bear-Bear *Beginning Consonants* **Bb, Hh, Mm, Vv** — 9

What's That Sound? *Beginning Consonants* **Bb, Pp, Rr, Ww, Yy, Zz** — 10

Fill It Up! *Beginning Consonants* **Bb, Jj, Ww** — 11

Letter Match *Beginning Consonants* — 12

Whose Toy Is It? *Beginning Consonants* **Dd, Rr, Zz** — 13

Picture This *Beginning Consonants* **Bb, Dd, Ff, Rr** — 14

Make Your Own Story *Beginning Consonants* **Cc, Tt** — 15

The Alphabet Zoo Game *Beginning Consonants* — 16–17

Make Your Own Bookmarks *Beginning Consonants* **Gg, Kk, Nn** — 18

Hidden Letters *Beginning Consonants* **Gg, Kk, Ll, Ss, Vv** — 19

Show What You Know *Standardized Test-taking Skills* — 20

Take-Home Book *The News at the Zoo* — 21–22

Classroom Fun *Group Games and Activities* — 23–25

Instant Activities *More Ideas for Quick and Easy Practice* — 26–27

Consonant Cards — 28

Word Bank — 29

Word/Picture Card Set — 30–31

Observation Checklist — 32

Using "Fun With Phonics"

Fun With Phonics! is a set of hands-on activity resource books that make phonics instruction easy and fun for you and the children in your classroom. Following are some ideas to help you get the most out of *Fun With Phonics!*

Classroom Management

Reproducibles Reproducible pages 7–19 offer a variety of individual and partner activities.

Directions You may wish to go over the directions with children and verify that they can identify all picture cues before they begin independent work.

Games When children play partner games, you may want to circulate in order to monitor that responses are correct and procedures have been understood.

Working with the Poem

A poem on page 6 introduces the phonics element in this book, beginning consonants. Start by reading this poem aloud to children. Duplicate the poem so children can work with it in a variety of ways:

Echo Reading Recite the poem, line by line, acting out the poem as you go. Have children echo the words and imitate the action.

Visual Discrimination Write the poem on a chart. Ask volunteers to circle each consonant letter and a word that begins with the same beginning consonant, such as *D, Duck.*

Dramatization Assign one line per child, and have children perform a dramatic reading of the poem. You may prefer to have children learn their assigned lines by heart. Encourage the child playing letter *B* to make a very dramatic appearance!

Connecting School and Home

The Family Letter on page 5 can be sent home to encourage families to reinforce what children are learning. Children will also enjoy sharing the Take-Home Book on pages 21–22. You can cut and fold these booklets ahead of time, or invite children to participate in the process. You may also mount the pages on heavier stock and place the Take-Home Book in your classroom library.

Word Card Sets

Pages 30–31 of this book contain matching sets of Word and Picture Cards drawn from the vocabulary presented in this book. You may wish to mount these on heavier stock as a classroom resource. You may also wish to duplicate and distribute them to children for use in matching and sorting activities. Each child can use a large envelope to store the cards. Each title in the *Fun with Phonics!* series contains a new set of thirty-two Word/Picture Cards.

Assessment

Page 20, Show What You Know, provides children with targeted practice in standardized test-taking skills, using the content presented in this book in the assessment items. The Observation Checklist on page 32 gives you an informal assessment tool.

Beginning Consonants © Scholastic Inc.

Dear Family,

Your child is learning in school about beginning consonants.

boat   **k**ey

Learning letters and sounds is an essential step in learning to read. You may enjoy sharing some or all of the following activities with your child.

Home Labels

Use sticky notes to label familiar items in your home with the beginning consonant of their names. Encourage your child to read these labels and to write or dictate labels for other home objects.

Letter Hunt

Choose a letter of the day and help your child look around the house for objects whose names begin with that letter. Invite other members of the family to join in the hunt. Post a list of items you have all found.

Reading Together

To practice recognizing beginning consonants, go over your child's Take-Home Book, "The News at the Zoo." Ask your child to point out or circle the beginning consonant in the name of each animal in the story and say it out loud.

You may also wish to look for the following books at your local library:

Happy, Hiding Hippos

Babette McCarthy

The Piggy in the Middle

Charlotte Pomerantz

Sincerely,

Name _____

Letters on the Run

I'm Afraid! called A.
Duck Down! said D.
Go on! Go on! cried letter G.
N and O just shouted NO!
P Paused, but Q was Quick to go.
Yipes! said Y, Zipping close to Z . . .
Unless I'm wrong, here comes a B!
BUZZZZZ!

Directions: Read the poem to the class once or twice. The next time you read, have children raise their hands or stand up each time they hear the name of an alphabet letter in the poem. See page 4, "Working with the Poem," for more ideas.

Roll-a-Letter

Here's a rainy day word game to make and play.

Fold line →

Hh

Pp

Jj

Ff

Ww

Nn

Directions: Have children play this game in pairs or small groups. First, make up the letter cube. Glue the page to lightweight cardboard and cut out the cube. Fold it and tape it together. Have children take turns rolling the cube. Tell them to name the letter that shows on top, as well as another word that begins with the same sound/letter. A child receives one point for each new word named. The first player to have five points wins the game.

Name _____

Gift Boxes

It's party time! Draw a gift in each box.

Directions: Review the letters and their sounds. Instruct children to draw a gift in each box whose name begins with the sound on the tag. Children dictate or write the name of each gift on the line.

Name _____

Bear-Bear

It's cold outside. Cut out the clothes. Dress Bear-Bear.

Directions: Have children cut out the squares and paste them on the bear, matching beginning sounds and letters. Then have them color Bear-Bear and his clothes.

Name _____

What's That Sound?

| Bb | Pp | ~~Rr~~ | Ww | Yy | ~~Zz~~ |

Directions: Go over the picture names with children. Tell them to say each name aloud, choose the letter from the letter box that stands for the beginning sound of the name, and write it on the line in the speech bubble. Finally, have children color the page.

Beginning Consonants **Bb, Pp, Rr, Ww, Yy, Zz**

Name _____

Fill It Up!

Fill up the containers.

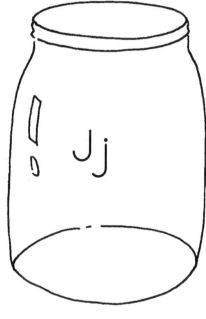

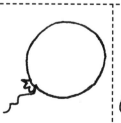     

Directions: Instruct the children to cut out the squares, say the names of the items to themselves, and match them with the container whose name begins with the same sound. Have them paste the squares in the correct containers.

Letter Match

Find out who
is acting silly.

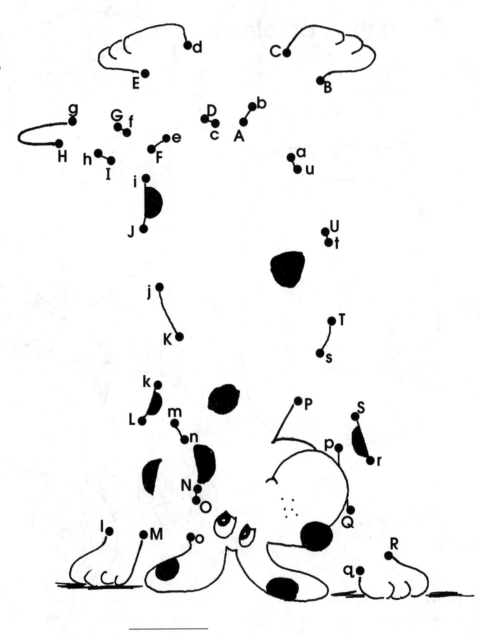

The _____ og is on his _____ ead.

Directions: Ask children to look for letter matches and to draw lines between the matching capital and lowercase letters. When they have completed the picture, they can complete the sentence by adding beginning consonants. Then encourage children to color in the picture.

Whose Toy Is It?

It's time to play!

_____ adio

_____ ebra

_____ oll

Dan

Rosa

Zeb

_____ uck

_____ oo

_____ obot

Directions: Read the names on the children's T-shirts aloud. Explain that each child only plays with toys whose names begin with the same sound as his or her name. Have children write the appropriate consonant to complete the name of each toy. Then have children draw lines from each child to the matching toys.

Name _____

Picture This

What belongs in each box?

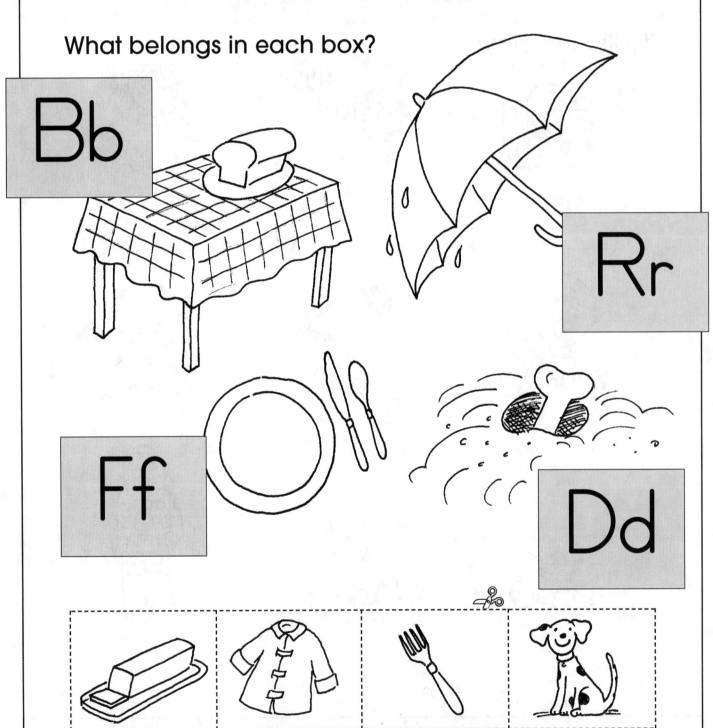

Directions: Ask the children to look over the page, read the letters in each box, and brainstorm what might belong in each picture. Then have children cut out the small pictures, say the name of each picture, and paste each one where it belongs.

Name _____

Make Your Own Story

Tt

Cc

Directions: This activity can be completed individually or in pairs. Talk about the pictures with the children. Have them cut out the story pieces for each letter, move them around, talk about them, and make up a story. Encourage children to paste their pictures on a piece of paper in story sequence. Be sure they understand that they don't have to use all the pieces. Ask volunteers to tell their stories to the class.

The Alphabet Zoo Game

This zoo is empty. Can you fill it up?

Bb	Cc	Dd	Ff	Gg
Ww				Hh
Xx		Start Here		Jj
Vv	Yy		Zz	Kk
Tt		Start Here		Ll
Ss				Free Turn
Rr	Qq	Pp	Nn	Mm

Beginning Consonants © Scholastic Inc.

bat	camel	deer
fish	gorilla	hippo
jellyfish	kangaroo	lion
monkey	newt	panda
quail	rabbit	swan
tiger	vulture	walrus
ox	yak	zebra

Directions: This game may be played by two or three players. You will need a number cube and one small distinguishable marker for each player. Go over the animal names with children. Have children cut out the animal cards, and place their markers in the center of the gameboard. Players deal out all the animal squares. They take turns rolling the number cube and moving their markers in any direction. If a player lands on a letter for which he or she has a matching animal card, the card is placed on the letter. The first player to place all of his or her animal cards wins the game. Individual children may also play the game, pasting the animal squares on the board until the board is complete.

Make Your Own Bookmarks

Make these bookmarks. Then use one as you read a book.

Directions: Have children cut out the boxes and paste them on the bookmark that matches the beginning consonant sound. Encourage children to use the bookmarks in school and to take one home to use with library books.

Hidden Letters

B, C, D, F, G, H, J, K, L, M, N, P, Q, R, S, T, V, W, X, Y, Z

Directions: Look over the pictures with children. Tell them to say the name of each picture aloud, and then look within the picture for the hidden letters that stand for the beginning sound of that name. Have children circle the hidden letters and then write the letters on the lines. Encourage children to create their own hidden letters picture in the empty box.

Beginning Consonants: **Gg, Kk, Ll, Ss, Vv**

Show What You Know

Say the name of each picture. Fill in the circle next to the letter that stands for the missing sound. Write the letter on the line.

1. _____ _____ _____ uck	○ d ○ b ○ y	2. _____ _____ _____ ueen	○ q ○ x ○ p	3. _____ _____ _____ est	○ v ○ w ○ t
4. _____ _____ _____ at	○ b ○ p ○ h	5. _____ _____ _____ at	○ g ○ c ○ j	6. _____ _____ _____ ish	○ p ○ f ○ d
7. _____ _____ _____ ite	○ l ○ k ○ h	8. _____ _____ _____ ebra	○ x ○ z ○ y	9. _____ _____ _____ ope	○ r ○ n ○ m
10. _____ _____ _____ ape	○ t ○ l ○ h	11. _____ _____ _____ oat	○ g ○ r ○ s	12. _____ _____ _____ ike	○ r ○ b ○ j

Directions: Go over the instructions with children, showing them how to fill in the circle.

The News at the Zoo

Shh. Don't wake up baby!

Wake up, tiger.

Wake up, kangaroo.

Wake up, monkey.

2

Roar

7

Wake up, panda.

4

Wake up, camel.

5

Classroom Fun ·····

Beginning Consonants

Get Aboard the Consonant Train!

Make a big train with one car for each consonant. Each car can be a piece of brightly colored construction paper, with paper plate wheels and a letter written near the front of the car. Staple the sides and bottom of each car to a bigger piece of paper. Place the cars around the classroom at a height children can reach. As you study each consonant, children can draw pictures or cut out pictures from magazines to fill each car. Discuss the car contents with children occasionally to review each letter.

Consonant Quilt!

Assign each child a consonant, and distribute sheets of construction paper and other art materials. Ask children to write their assigned letter and decorate the sheet with pictures whose names begin with the sound of that letter. Cut out long strips of a contrasting color, to place between the pages. When you tape or staple all the letters together, you will have a consonant quilt to display in the hall or classroom.

B Is for Beanbag

Divide a large sheet of drawing paper into sections, and write a consonant letter in each section. Then challenge children to a beanbag toss. Have them take turns tossing the beanbag onto the paper. The child must say the name of the letter in the section the beanbag has landed in, along with a word that begins with that letter. Players earn one point for each new word.

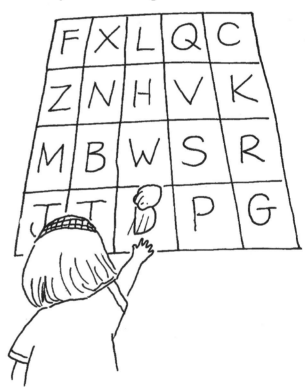

Tongue Twisters

With the class, brainstorm words that begin with a particular consonant letter. Write each word on a big index card. Let children take turns closing their eyes and rearranging the cards. Then read the words aloud in the random new tongue twisting order and have children attempt to say the words after you.

Classroom Fun

Play "OOPS!"

This game uses the consonant cards on page 28. Choose the letters you would like the children to review, at least 8 at a time. Have children play the game with partners. A child turns over the squares one at a time. As each letter is revealed, the child must name it and say a word that begins with that letter. If the child is successful, he or she can move to the next letter. If not, the other player writes a big O on a piece of paper. The object of the game is for one player to get through the whole stack of cards without making four mistakes and ending up with O-O-P-S!

Shopping Spree

Distribute consonant cards from page 28, one for each child. Challenge children to make a list of things they will buy whose names begin with that letter. Let them have fun expanding their purchases, as long as they use the letter correctly. For example, for the letter *Nn*, "new car" would be acceptable. See who can make the longest list.

Consonant Picture Dictionary

Work with children to make a consonant picture dictionary. Start with a simple photo album or a 3-ring binder with plastic insert pages. Set aside a page or two for each consonant. Place a cut-out consonant letter inside each section. Encourage children to make drawings or find pictures they can cut out of magazines whose names begin with that consonant. Have them continue to add pictures to the appropriate section in the consonant picture dictionary throughout the school year.

Consonant Charades

Divide the class into competing teams. Prepare index cards with letters and action words. You can get some ideas from the Word Bank on page 29. Here are some to try:

Ww—wash windows
Rr—row a boat
Vv—vacuum the room
Pp—paint a wall
Hh—hang out clothes

Distribute one card at a time to each team, and quietly help the team read the action words as necessary. Have the team act out the word, as the other team tries to guess what it is.

Letter Stories

Encourage children to tell and write "letter stories" independently, with partners, or in small groups. To help children practice letters and sounds, you may want to brainstorm words that begin with the target letter. Here are just a few story-starting ideas:

Letter L is Lost!
H has the Hiccups!
How can We Wake Up W?
D has Disappeared!
R Can't Stop Running
S Is So Silly!

Fish for Letters

Cut out fish shapes from colored paper or gift wrap. Write a consonant on each one. Clip a big paper clip to each fish. Place all the fish shapes in a box or paper plate. Then use a ruler and string to make a fishing pole. Tie a small magnet to the end of the string. Have children take turns fishing for letters. If a child can say the letter and think of a word that begins with the sound that letter stands for, he or she can keep the fish. The player with the most fish at the end of the game wins.

Consonant Baseball

Place four chairs around the room to serve as first base, second base, third base, and home plate. Organize the class into two teams. When the first team is "up," the first player sits at home plate. You are the pitcher: Write a consonant on the board. The player must then name the consonant and a word that begins with that letter/sound. If the player answers correctly, he or she moves to first base. If not, the side is out, and the other team is up. Teams make points when a player advances all the way around the bases. A player may take more than one base at a time by giving a two or even three-word answer, such as "B—baby boy."

Letters Checkers

Paste consonant letters on the black squares of a checkerboard. You can cover every square, or just a few. Two versions of each letter, one facing in each direction, will allow both players to see the letter equally well. Children play checkers as usual, but with one difference. Before moving to a square, they must be able to name the letter and its sound. To make the game a little more difficult, instruct players to name the letter, its sound, and two words that begin with that letter/sound.

Put This on File

Challenge the children to help you fill a file box with consonants. Bring in a cardboard file box with alphabet dividers, and remove the vowels. As you study letters in class, invite the children to find words and pictures whose names begin with that letter sound. You may want to post a copy of the Word Bank from page 29 for children's reference. Have children draw or cut and paste pictures on the file cards. When it's time for review, you can just pull out the cards for that letter.

Instant Activities

Mother May I Play "Mother, May I?" as usual, but with one twist. Before players can take a step, hop, or leap, they must correctly name a word that begins with the consonant letter of your choice.

I Spy Say, "I see something that begins with the letter *B*." Children guess until someone names the item. Then that child takes a turn at thinking of an "I Spy" object.

Shiny Consonants Pass out index cards. Assign each child a consonant letter. Have each child write the letter in glue and shake glitter on it. Display the shiny consonants on the chalk tray.

Ghost Letters Have each child trace a consonant letter on a partner's back. A correct guess means the partner gets a turn to trace a letter.

Consonant Riddles Pose riddles like the ones below. Tell children to use their imaginations. Ask them to pose new riddles to you and their classmates.
Which letter buzzes? *(B)*
Which letter is very wet? *(C)*
Which letters play music? *(DJ)*
Which letter has a shirt named after it? *(T)*
Which letter is a vegetable? *(P)*

Wiggle Worm Consonants Have four children lie on the floor. Instruct them to wiggle until they form a W. Then do the same with other letters.

Consonant Charades Act out a word for each consonant. Tell the class the beginning letter and challenge them to guess the word. (Examples are bounce for *B*, cough for *C*, dig for *D*, and so on.)

Old MacDonald Sing the classroom favorite, "Old MacDonald Had a Farm." Substitute letters and their sounds for the traditional animal names and sounds.

Letter Tag Distribute the consonant cards from page 28. Divide the class into two teams and have them line up on one side of the room. The first child on each team must place his or her letter next to something in the room that begins with that letter, then run back and tag the next child in line. The team that is first to place all of its letters correctly wins the game.

Categories Pick a category, such as animals or foods. See how many items in that category the class can think of that begin with certain letter sounds. For example, animals beginning with *P* might include pandas, parrots, pigs, and porcupines.

Match That Consonant Hold up an object. Ask children to say its name and the name of its beginning sound. Challenge children to find something else in the room that begins with the same sound.

"The Wheels on the Bus" Sing the popular song "The Wheels on the Bus." Ask children to help you come up with new verses that have repeating consonants, for example:
"The tubas on TV go toot, toot, toot..."
"The bees on the bus go buzz, buzz, buzz..."
"The worms in the wood go wiggle, wiggle, wiggle..."

Consonant Party Begin the game by saying, "Let's have a consonant party. I'll bring bananas to the party." The next person must offer to bring something that begins with another consonant, such as "raisins." If you want to make the game more challenging, ask players to answer cumulatively: "I'll bring bananas and raisins to the party."

"I Say . . ." Begin with all the children standing by their desks. Children take turns saying a word beginning with a consonant letter. For example, the first few children might say, "I say brown." "I say baby." "I say bear." "I say bee." When a child can't think of a word beginning with that letter, he or she sits down, and the game moves on to the next letter. The last child left standing wins the game.

Play "A My Name Is Alice." Children can take turns, going all the way through the alphabet.
"A my name is Alice. We live in Alaska. And we sell apples."
"B my name is Bonnie. We live in Boston. And we sell butter."

Consonant Cards

B	C	D	F	G
H	J	K	L	M
N	P	Q	R	S
T	V	W	X	Y
Z				

Directions: Cut out the letters. You may want to back them on cardboard or laminate them. Use them for a variety of games, including the games described in "Classroom Fun" and "Instant Activities."

Word Bank

Below is a list of words that you may use to illustrate words with beginning consonants. Some of these words are included in the Word/Picture Card set on pages 30–31. Ideas for using these cards and additional cards you may create yourself can be found in "Classroom Fun," pages 23–25.

———— **Beginning Consonants** ————

B	D	G	J	M	P	R	T	X
bag	deer	game	jacks	mail	paint	rain	tail	box
ball	desk	gas	jam	man	pan	rake	talk	fix
barn	dig	gate	jar	map	pat	rat	tape	fox
bat	dirt	gift	jeans	mat	pen	red	ten	mix
bed	dish	girl	jeep	match	pie	ring	tie	ox
bend	dive	go	jet	milk	pig	road	tip	six
bike	dog	goat	jog	mitten	pin	roll	toe	
bird	doll	golf	jug	moon	pour	rope	toy	**Y**
boy	door	goose	jump	mop	pull	rose	tub	yak
bug	down	gum		mouse	purse	rub		yam
bus	duck		**K**	mouth	push	run	**V**	yank
		H	key	mud			van	yard
C	**F**	hair	kid		**Qu**	**S**	vase	yawn
call	face	hand	kilt	**N**	quack	sail	vest	yarn
can	fall	hang	king	nail	quail	sand	vine	yellow
cap	fan	hat	kiss	neck	quart	sat	violin	yes
car	farm	head	kite	nest	queen	saw		yolk
cat	fence	hear		night	quilt	seven	**W**	
coat	fight	heart	**L**	nose		sing	wag	**Z**
comb	finger	hill	lamp	nurse		sink	wagon	zebra
cow	fire	hit	leaf	nut		six	walk	zig-zag
cut	fish	hole	leg			soap	watch	zipper
	five	hop	lick			sock	water	zoo
	foot	horn	line			soup	web	zoom
	four	house	lion			sun	wing	
	fox	hum	log				wink	
			look				wolf	

Word Cards

ball	cow	duck	fish
gum	hat	king	milk
nest	pig	queen	rope
sock	tie	wagon	zebra

Picture Cards

Observation Checklist

Name	Identifies consonants	Matches upper- and lowercase letters	Associates letters and sounds	Names words beginning with consonant letters	Writes consonants correctly

Phonemic Awareness

E=Excellent   G=Good   N=Needs Improvement   R=Reteach